Porn-Anti-Porn

by Harold Jaffe

D1571729

Books by Harold Jaffe

Porn-anti-Porn
Goosestep (fictions & docufictions)
Sacred Outcast: Dispatches from India
Death Café (fictions & docufictions)
Induced Coma: 50 & 100-Word Stories
Othello Blues (novel)
Revolutionary Brain (essays/quasi-essays)
OD (docufictions)
Paris 60 (travel)
Anti-Twitter: 150 50-Word Stories
Jesus Coyote (novel)
Beyond the Techno-Cave (non-fiction)
Terror-Dot-Gov (docufictions)
15 Serial Killers (docufictions)
Son of Sam (docufiction)
Nazis, Sharks & Serial Killers (non-fiction)
False Positive (docufictions)
Sex for the Millennium (extreme tales)
Straight Razor (stories)
Eros Anti-Eros (fictions)
Madonna and Other Spectacles (fictions)
Beasts (fictions)
Dos Indios (novel)
Mourning Crazy Horse (stories)
Mole's Pity (novel)

Porn-Anti-Porn

by Harold Jaffe

Journal of Experimental Fiction 81

JEF Books/Depth Charge Publishing
Aurora, Illinois

Cover Design by Norman Conquest
Illustrations by Thomas Gresham

ISBN 1-884097-81-2
ISBN-13 978-1-884097-81-2

ISSN 1084-547X

This volume is volume 81 of
The Journal of Experimental Fiction

JEF Books/Depth Charge Publishing
The Foremost in Innovative Fiction
Experimentalfiction.com

JEF Books are distributed
to the book trade by SPD: Small Press Distribution
and to the academic journal market by EBSCO

ACKNOWLEDGEMENTS

Gratitude to Sebastian Bennett, Shane Roeschlein, Thomas Gresham, Stephen-Paul Martin, Joan Raymond, and Andy O'Clancy for reading and commenting on this volume in manuscript

PORN HUB CLAIMED MORE THAN 82 MILLION VISITORS A DAY IN 2017, WHICH AMOUNTS TO NEARLY 29 BILLION VISITORS A YEAR.

THE global-wide porn culture online, which enlists tens of thousands of sexual participants, has not received careful attention. Viewers tend to be damning, indifferent, or, especially if they are young, exhilarated.

Pornography exists cheek-by-jowl with a faux-moral culture to which it seems utterly opposed. The vast online porn culture empire, owned by many of the same industries who tout morality or "political correctness" offline, such as Disney and Fox, points to a schizoid division in global at-large culture: parallel narratives, governed by the same corporations, with the online porn narrative sexually inverting in virtually every instance its own offline pieties.

Offline, #MeToo primarily addresses males in power who sexually abuse females "under" them. Online, teenage girls sexually assault and abuse their fathers and "superiors." Offline, racism is condemned; online, it is a staple, with Asian girls and virile black young men, for example, objectified in graphic racist terms. Offline, the female body has been rendered into private property. No trespassing! Online, the female body belongs to the hyper-assertive hetero male, or at the very least is communal property.

The Machiavellian corporations that produce both the videos online and diametrically opposed discourse offline rake in the easy billions.

But hasn't this always been the sexual dialectic? The pornographer's best friend is the censor. The moralizing politician or priest who rails against sin and sexual deviation is abusing young assistants and choir boys. That *is* an ongoing dialectic, perhaps especially in the US where, for example, seductive young women, are "for sale" commercially but in fact are off-limits. However, online their for-sale seductiveness is transfigured into utterly available tattooed sirens.

The point is that the stakes of the online-offline split now are far more crucial than before, because it has much to do with "realities" in mortal conflict: what remains of the "real" world at war with the ever-burgeoning hyper-reality of tech-life.

My "examination" of the pornography phenomenon describes a wide arc.

A scholar wrote some time ago that for her the pornographic was epitomized when viewing on TV President George W. Bush vomit into the lap of a visiting dignitary at an official state dinner, and this volume addresses similarly extended notions of pornography.

Among other stratagems, I move from country to country. Granting the corporate porn site owners' rank opportunism, there is about the naked body in passion, or even simulated passion, less mediation than that same body offline and socially constructed. That is, naked Kamasutra participants tell us more about themselves and the country they in effect represent than we'd learn otherwise. Hence I provide a view of the US, Japan, China, France, Germany, Thailand, the UK, Russia, the Czech Republic, etc, that is both intimate and ideologically revealing.

Porn-anti-Porn is descriptive, but also analytical and "creative." Critical exposition, miniature narratives, pastiche, and dialogues are displayed in various tonalities, always with brevity. A number of the texts were published items which I've plundered and "treated" to reveal subtexts and obscured ideologies. The original venues of these treated texts--called "docufiction"--are listed on the final page under "Sources."

CONTENTS

No life on earth can be hid from our dreaming

DANCE

Bruno Bettelheim recounts the story of a young Jewess, formerly a gifted dancer, imprisoned in Auschwitz. Stripped naked, with her head shaved, in a queue with other Jewish girls and women stripped, shaved, en-route to the gas, the Gestapo officer addresses her. "I am informed that you were a dancer. Dance for me." Without hesitation she commences to dance deliberately, seductively, gliding toward the mesmerized Nazi officer. Removing the luger from his holster she shoots him dead.

.

VAN PORN

One guy wanted us to buy a van, have my wife and a couple other girls drive around in it for 8 days wearing a bra but no panties, smoke cigarettes in the van, pee and poop in the van, and at the end of the week we drive it out into the desert and blow it up.

He sent us pics of the exact van he had in mind.

PORN STAR

Is it what you expected?

What?

Online porn.

I've only been in it for 3 months.

Which is a lifetime online. That shit jumps.

I've done 40 different vids in 3 months.

Do you get turned on in front of the lights & camera & shit?

You don't, you're out of a job.

Can't fake it?

Not with that technology. Those closeups.

Your faves? Male, female, trans, mutliples, machine sex, face-sitting, BBC, pegging, bukkake?

We being bugged?

Absolutely.

I love 'em all. Together or apart.

You're young, but you lose it quick in this biz.
What do you mean to do when you're out of porn?

Look for work.

COUVADE

Lie on the shelf above me, experience my labor and have my baby.

After I conceive we will exchange places, I will experience your labor, have your baby.

After we both conceive we will make love deliriously.

WELL-ENDOWED

A 16-year-old secretly painted an 80 foot penis on the roof of his parents' 18 million dollar mansion in Beverly Hills.

It was there for more than a year before his parents discovered it.

BUKKAKE

Bukkake (ブッカケ) Literally "splash" in Japanese.

Refers to ejaculating onto another person in pornography.

A common curtain closer in Western porn; a genre of its own in Japan.

There's a Japanese dish named bukkake soba / don't get the two "dishes" confused.

Cat Café--A place people go to pet cats.

G-SPOT

Advisory to males: Stop searching for the G-spot.
First, it's inappropriate to use terms for the female body
named after males. The G- or Gräfenberg spot was
named after the German gynecologist Ernst
Gräfenberg, who also developed the IUD.
Second, the G-spot simply does not exist--at least not
in the magical push-button way of male fantasies.

JUST LIKE GIN

I've lived with my stepfather for eight years.

When I was young he was ok but the older I get the more we resent each other.

He can be aggressive, but what really pisses me off is he watches porn all the time, usually when my mum is out.

My sister and I got used to walking past the living room and hearing loud female moans.

I am 19 now, my sister has left home, and I feel more alone and disgusted than ever.

I tell my mum but all she says is "It's an addiction just like gin."

MEN

My husband was always tactile and affectionate but rarely wanted to have sex even in the early stages of our relationship. He eventually stopped altogether and was vague about the reasons. I begged him to have therapy, and he agreed, but never started.

I felt undesired and undesirable and eventually stopped thinking about sex. But then, after three decades, the other shoe finally dropped--he announced he was gay and left.

That was my explanation, but it was a bitter pill. Why on earth had he married me, been unfaithful and cheated me out of a sex life? He does not seem to know.

I'm 62 now and keen to make up for lost time. Nor has long abstinence affected my ability to enjoy sex. With less concern about appearance and performance and, surprisingly, no lack of willing partners, the act itself is easier to negotiate than when I was younger.

Is it possible to trust men again? *You tell me.*

BUTTPLUG

I placed a buttplug in Alabama,
Sovereign upon a hill.
It made the strip malls surround that hill.

Malls rose up,
No longer stupid.
The buttplug was comfy in any sphere.

It took dominion everywhere.
It did not give of Twitter, Goog, or Crimson Tide football,
Like nothing else in Alabama.

E-Sx

I'm feeling horny &
want to sext with a cute laid back guy
Msg me back &
I'll txt U some kool hot pix.

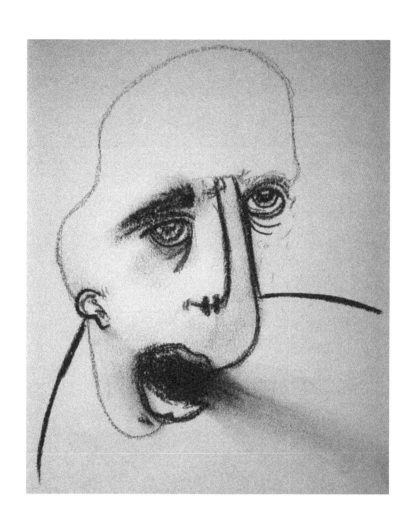

ORAL SEX

produces a virus that causes tongue cancer.

The risk is nine-and-a-half times higher for those who have had oral sex with more than six partners.

However, oral sex participants should understand that tongue cancer is uncommon, and contracting the virus will rarely signal tongue cancer.

ABSINTHE

Is a different Jesus which is why it is prohibited.

Opium is a different Buddha which is why "Science" has maintained its toxicity while diminishing the euphoria.

Kief is purest in Morocco which means *jihad* which is why it is prohibited.

Ayahuasca, called **Yage,** is for impoverished Peruvian *Indios* and dotcom hyper-wealthy US "adventurers."

Ecstasy has been cut with Drano for the "rave" mob, which means more delirium / less sex.

Peyote is consigned to leftover Native Americans.

Morphine for dying humans is under assault because dying must spell grief for patients and $$$ for medical care.

Psilocybin is for old hippies who still sex but lack faith in the **Darkweb.**

Cannabis with carcinogenic additives will be widely available as soon as Monsanto seals the deal.

CARTWHEEL IN OKLAHOMA

Police report that a Pawhuska, Oklahoma substitute teacher wasn't wearing underwear when she did a cartwheel in front of 12-year-old students, exposing her genitals and buttocks to the class.

KOSHER KUSH

Is an Indica hybrid with the distinction of being the first commercial strain blessed by a Rabbi.

The Rabbi lives in Texarkana.

The blessing is reported to bring both bliss and tranquility.

The strain produces a potent, lazy body buzz that leaves novice users deeply sedated, while elevating their moods with its sativa-based cerebral effects.

The user suddenly feels super sexy.

Caution should be exercised as the sleepiness can overwhelm.

This same sleepiness makes Kosher Kush effective for treating insomnia and restlessness caused by stress.

Patients in pain may also find it helpful due to its numbing body effects.

Dry eyes and mouth, paranoia, vertigo, and anxiety are potential downsides of this strain.

On the other hand, downsides have been recorded as pleasurable, even erotic, when under the influence of Kosher Kush.

WITHOUT

IED. Improvised Explosive Device.

Iraq, 2005. Blast blew them off, but my penis survived.

No point in a penis without testicles.

I had a girlfriend, but she dumped me.

No one since.

The Army paid for me to get hormone replacement therapy.

It turned me into a wolf-man with a painfully erect penis, but I also became fat and crazy violent and lost my hair.

So they switched me to a "safer" testosterone and I've been completely impotent.

I started watching porn but it only reinforced my isolation.

I began visiting escort girls for a kiss and a squeeze, lying with them in my arms wearing my underpants.

I tried phone sex, pretending to ejaculate.

I've fantasized about fantasies, different versions of

virile masculinity.

I began making deliberately inept passes at pretty women, imagining their inevitable rejection had nothing to do with my impotence.

Another sham pantomime.

That's it, I'm a sexual zero.

I admire a woman abstractly, want her desperately, but with no outlet for the surge.

I've tried to teach myself to repress dangerous emotions.

But I'm only 37.

The anguish doesn't stop.

ALABAMA

How hard is my dick?

Tungsten steel.

Just one thing harder than Tungsten steel.

My love for Jesus.

Can I get an amen?

WEAK CHIN

It started like teen relationships do--a boy tracking a girl on Instagram. **Baddude69** claimed to be a 15-year-old from Yonkers & his profile pic showed chiseled abs. She was an impressionable 14-year-old living with her father in Staten Island.

Instagram led to texting which led to an online friendship. Soon they were boyfriend & girlfriend expressing their love over text; they never met in non-tech time.

Their chats were frequent & explicit, the boy obsessed with sex and trading raunchy selfies, which he'd provide without warning. After months of pressing her to return the favor, she'd had it. She decided to break up but her boyfriend wouldn't let her without the porn selfies he craved.

When she refused to comply, he threatened to show her father the couple's explicit chats, as well as an earlier, soft-core selfie she'd sent him.

She texted him: I told you a bunch of times when we were dating I don't like those pics & now you are threatening me that if I don't send you them you'll send my dad the ones I sent you before? *My life is ruined.*

What she didn't know, authorities say now, was a secret so bizarre that it defies imagination: The "teenage boy" making threats & going on about sex online was, in reality, the girl's father--a 44-year--old accountant with a weak chin living under the same roof as the teen he was tormenting.

LYNCH HIM

It is the Time of AIDS.

A middle-aged male with the HIV virus checks into a hotel in San Diego and is soon going out with young men with whom he is likely having sex.

One young man, questioned afterwards, says it was mutual masturbation.

Another says the man blew him and paid him for it.

Once it is uncovered and broadcast that a middle-aged male with HIV (construed as equivalent to AIDS) was preying on young men the cry was "Lynch Him."

No official paused to consider whether the sex the man was having with the young men was capable of transmitting AIDS or any other STD.

The man hangs himself before he can be lynched.

None of his younger partners become infected.

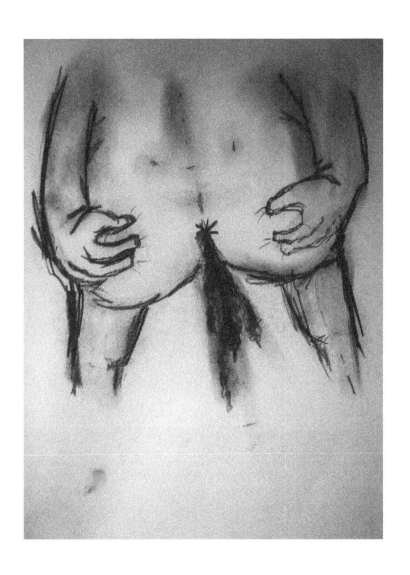

ASSHOLE POLLOCHTICS

It is the time of AIDS.

You are an infected homosexual male artist.

Get naked, set the empty canvas between your legs.

Spray colored (non-toxic) paint from your anus onto the canvas Jackson Pollock style.

BILLBOARDS

A PR agent in Tokyo is trying to get attention in the advertisement-saturated capital by placing adverts on young women's thighs.

Participants, who must be over 18, are recommended to wear miniskirts and long socks to draw attention to the campaigns.

More than 7,000 young women already registered to give up their skin to become "billboards."

GREEN MONKEY

Take the asshole. 20 years ago it was off-off-limits because of its association with the "sodomy" that produced that devil's disease AIDS.
The Green Monkey transmitted the disease to black Africans who then transmitted it to globetrotting homosexuals.
The result is written on subway toilet walls.
So declared the gospel according to Jesse Helms.

Today the asshole is *comme il faut*.
Every female strip scene must display the asshole with its delicate striations and peekaboo cleft.
Note the mediation of bleach.
White fems who act in porn will often bleach their asshole area for an all-white look.
It helps pay the bills.

BENTLEY

Hello beautiful how you doing today?

My name is Bentley from the US.

I'm in Afghan right now fighting ISIS.

I want to get to know you better.

I consider myself an easy-going guy.

I am looking for a relationship where I feel loved.

Please tell me about yourself.

Hope to hear from you soon.

--Bentley

COLLEGE CAMPUS 2018

Male & female student have a drunken hookup.

Male wakes up terrified fem's going to file a sexual misconduct complaint.

Male contacts the Title IX office & beats fem to the punch.

Female is found guilty & suspended.

ISIS SEX SLAVES

Markets selling sex slaves are common in territory controlled by ISIS in Iraq and Syria, and the ISIS franchise in Libya has also played a role in sex trafficking.

One account describes how ISIS members pinch the chests of girls to determine whether they have breasts.

With breasts they are raped, then murdered if the sex is unsatisfactory.

Without breasts they are examined three months later.

ANA

A man faces jail after being convicted of luring other men into having sex by posing as a woman named Ana.

Duarte Xavier used online dating sites to contact 7 heterosexual men and deployed various ruses, including telling them he was married and wanted to engage in role play, to convince them to wear blindfolds before engaging in perverted sexual acts.

Police said Xavier's 7 victims, all of whom initially believed he was female, were left "traumatized" by his crimes, which they described as "unique in their depravity".

PORN ADDICT

So you're a porn addict.

I look at porn online.

Frequently?

When I feel like it.

You're hetero. You date females. Has your porn addiction helped or hindered your sex life offline?

Helped.

You don't feel equipment-shamed, seeing all those stunt dicks go at it?

I get ideas.

Example?

*Sexual positions. **Kamsutra** stuff. Shit comes right at you.*

You look supple. For an older dude. What other ideas do you get?

Fetish. I've seen appealing—to me—fetish action I never considered before.

Example?

Hang on. Are we being bugged?

What a question! Absolutely.

I'm a clean machine. I'm addicted to condoms and the missionary position.

PORN ADDICT

"If I'm compelled to rummage around in the dumpster at 3 am for a porn DVD, there's something wrong in my brain, I'm ill … it's mental illness, right?"

No. You're addicted to rummaging in the dumpster at 3 am for a porn DVD, is all.

MONGO MASSAGE TIPS

Another prob is climaxing too early in the session with your masseuse beating on your noodle and more than 30 minutes left on the clock.

Try beating off *before* coming to the parlor, not the exact moment before you come in, two or three hours before, and get your second finish of the day, but with some assistance. You'll last longer plus you won't leave that much cum for your masseuse to clean up.

My other recommendation, which I only rec if you're not gonna be actually scoring a FS with the provider, is take the ugliest chick they got. Okay, you're laughing and pointing at the screen: "Wow Mongo gets it on with the uggo bitches?" Hear me out: if you get a Handy Mandy from a not-so-pretty Mandy, won't it take longer for you to finish? Does for me, plus I get more bang for my buck.

Anyways, you can probably get away with asking for more massage after the happy stuff. It wouldn't be an ending, more like a happy in-between, you feel me? The session doesn't have to be a full 30 minutes of wrist motion action.

SEVER

How long would you wish a man who severed your penis and flushed it down the toilet to remain in jail? Before you decide, know that you slept with his wife (before he severed your penis).
Will this scenario inspire you to forgive the man who severed your penis?

Reports have it that the man who severed and flushed the penis apologized to his victim. The victim in turn apologized to the man for having slept with his wife.

NEUROLAW

Neurolaw experts have been discussing whether medication could affect a human's brain to the extent where his/her sexual inclinations change or suddenly present in bizarre ways.

Consider former Tasmanian MP Clovis Kath, 62, convicted of unlawful intercourse with a 15-year-old in 2012.

Though Kath pleaded guilty it was brought forward that his Parkinson's medication--a dopamine agonist--had directly caused his hypersexuality.

While taking this medication, Kath, previously boring and semi-impotent, was never not erect, and while engorged uncovered an extraordinarily broad range of sexual interests he'd never demonstrated before-- eXXXtreme fetish porn, pubescent girls, boys, bots, girlyboys.

When Kath ceased taking the medication those interests vanished virtually overnight, he resumed being boring and semi-impotent, hence was cured of the medication-induced changes to his brain responsible for his offensive behavior.

Kath's conviction was not overturned. He was sentenced to five-and-a-half years.

WESTCOAST MASSAGE

Hello I would like to see you for enjoy

We are Asia

Very sure I and my friend not old not fat

Professional

Prostate milking with request

We open right now

Text

AI

Can calculate whether humans are gay or straight based on photos of their faces.

The algorithm can distinguish between adult gay and straight males 89% of the time and between lesbians and straight females 81% of the time.

Gay males and females tend to have "gender-atypical" features, expressions and grooming styles; specifically, gay males appear more feminine and gay females more masculine.

Gay males have narrower jaws, longer noses and larger foreheads than straight males. Gay females have larger jaws and smaller foreheads than straight females.

These alleged findings are uncomfortable. With billions of facial images stored on social media sites and in government databases that info could be used and abused to detect people's sexual orientation without their consent.

ARO

The thought of not feeling romance may seem a little strange. For Jena, a 22-year-old "genius" at a local Apple store, it is natural. She is part of an exponentially growing community who identify as "aromantic," or ARO.

 "For me, ARO is simply not having any romantic attraction," Jena says. "It's not *not* having feelings."

Some AROs realize their identity as early as puberty. "I've identified as ARO since high school kids started getting into relationships," an aromantic woman, who wished to remain anonymous, says. "I was like 'What's the big deal?'"

For others, ARO came later. Noralee, a 30-year-old divorced parent of two and aspiring computer technician, realized only after she started dating again. "My friend set me up with a male. He was nice, good looking, and kind of pressed all the buttons. In three weeks I felt nothing for him. Zilch. After that, looking back over the years of dating. I realized that even when dating someone nice, I never felt more than a mild comfort."

Maryrose struggled with the concept of aromanticism before she became comfortable. "Coming to terms with it was hard. I had to rethink every [mis]conception I had about love, whether romantic, sexual or platonic. "

Are all AROS asexual? "Online aromantic communities seem asexual by default," says Mark Lemming, a 27-year-old ARO from Utah. Lemming founded a Facebook "herd" for AROs who *do* feel sexual attraction. "The reaction has been overwhelmingly positive. I never advertised my herd," says Lemming, "[but] it is growing real, real fast."

There are a wide variety of Facebook pages from *Aromantic Non-Asexuals* to *Happily Aromantic*, as well as blogs devoted to *Aromanticism* on Tumblr. Their members are said to number in the thousands. While predominantly young, the AROS have variable backgrounds, gender identities and sexual orientations.

Lemming: "I am happy the Net is making it easy to find and create communities with similar disinterest in romance. Folks seem ecstatic to realize there are others like them when they find my herd."

Online communities help AROs overcome the stigma attached to rejecting romance. "People think that I 'just haven't met the right person', which is, of course, not true," says Noralee. "I *have* found the right person—myself."

AROs are routinely accused of delusion and heartlessness. Maryrose insists that's not the case: "I'm not cold or a prude. I just don't feel romantic feelings for anyone. I still have a huge, sensitive heart. I watch Hallmark movies about true love and marriage and cry!" One of her favorite films is the 1987 fantasy *The Princess Bride*.

Where then does the stigma come from? "An obsession with romantic love is clearly the norm in western culture," Lemming says. "People imagine romantic love is superior to all other forms of human connection."

Despite the intense social pressure to experience romance, AROS have one message: it is OK if you don't. Maryrose: "I will maybe never fall in love, I will never get married, I may spend the rest of my life alone with my hundreds of cats in my big country house--but I am not mad or messed up about it."

MINT TEA

Q. I am a 34-year-old woman with a 53-year-old husband. I love him dearly but he has ED, and in the last year his sex drive has dropped as well. I always let him approach me for sex as the other way round doesn't work. We usually make love once a month although I would prefer daily or at least once a week. I think about sex with him a lot.

I was fascinated to read that mint tea might dampen sexual interest, so I tried it. With a cup of mint tea morning and evening I soon lost my constant nagging desire. I am so thrilled.

A. Spearmint tea (*Mentha spicata*) can lower testosterone levels. A woman may find this will help reduce her sex drive. Many women feel desperate and alone dealing with a "taboo issue." Which is why this link has become popular with so many women who have shared their feelings and frustrations.

We invite you to visit the page to appreciate the despair this problem has created for so many women.

LEAP YEAR

In my 20s I lived with a man my age but he was a controlling alcoholic. The sex dropped to twice a year and he didn't like me masturbating. I tried counseling but it didn't work.

I left three years later and played the field. I met a lot of guys and took a shine to a 70-year-old. We did the dirty that night. He was retired and said if I lived with him I could have sex whenever I wanted. I moved in and we were intimate every night and morning, during the day on weekends, and all day and night on Leap Year.

After we split I didn't want a live-in relationship but became used to daily orgasms and sex a dozen times a week. I dated guys but believe it or not none was as good as my 70-year-old. I split my time between half-a-dozen and had a reliable stable of male company, plus backup. They all love being with me.

Men make love differently, but I find it easy to remember how to be with each one; their particular embrace reminds me. I've been sexing for 11 years with one man and 6 years with the most recent.

One is 13 years older than me, some are half my age. I have sex 12 or 15 times a week.

I don't know if this is "normal," but it feels right and that's all I care about.

ALL-FEMALE ANT

An Amazonian ant (*Myocepurus smithii*) has dispensed with sex altogether and developed into an all-female species.

The singular species reproduce via cloning--the queen ants replicate themselves to produce genetically identical daughters.

The finding of the ants' "World Without Sex" is published in the *Proceedings of the Royal Society*.

CURE GAYS

A proposal to treat homosexuality medically has been critically received.

A London-based conference headlines an American "psychoneurologist" who claims to help unhappy homosexuals become gleeful heteros virtually overnight without surgery by "tapping" the cluster of cells in the "preoptic area of the human hypothalamus."

The Royal College of Psychiatrists (UK), objects, claiming there is no firm evidence the treatment works; moreover, it may create a setting in which gender discrimination flourishes.

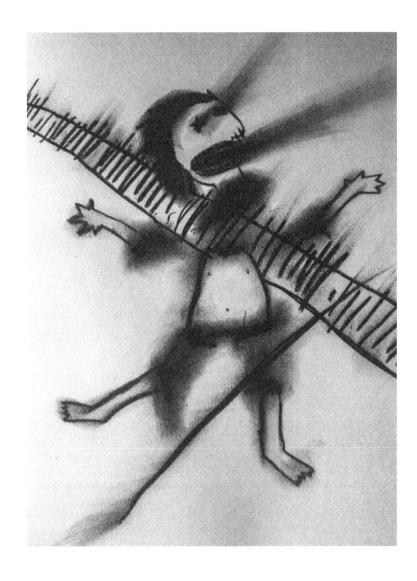

WATCHING

The mother of a 10-year-old girl found dead and dismembered in her New Mexico home told police she sought men online to sexually assault her daughter.

The *Albuquerque Journal* reports that Dolores-Jean Martens told police she set up encounters with at least five men. The child's brutal death sparked vigils and outcry across New Mexico.

According to warrants obtained by the *Journal*, Martens said she didn't do it for the money. She set up the sexual assaults because she enjoyed watching.

Police found the child's dismembered body last month inside the Albuquerque apartment she shared with her mother.

BEARD OIL

Never thought of myself as a beard oil kind of guy.
Boy, was I missing out, writes Duane in Nashville.
This stuff tames my unruly man hedge into a silky
smooth bowl of cream spinach.

Made of olive, hazelnut, rosemary, CBD and Vitamin E.
4 big aromas: Dirt, Lumberjack, Sexy, Mansweat.

EPISTEMOLOGY

#Pornography everywhere & climate change

#Climate change everywhere & smartphones

#Smartphones everywhere & money-lust

#Money-lust everywhere & climate change

#Climate Change everywhere & entertainment

#Entertainment everywhere & moralisms

#Moralisms everywhere & pornography

#Pornography everywhere & cruelty

Question: How cruel is the cruelty?

Beyond forgiveness.

SEX WORKER

Despite her defiant cheerfulness, she doesn't gloss over the industry's brutal sides. Many of her colleagues are mothers who see clients when their children are at school, nudged into prostitution as they battle the consequences of benefit cuts and job losses.

--I don't push the happy hooker myth. You'd be surprised at the time I spend talking women out of going into the industry. It's a rough environment. It can make or break you. Some women make it. I know because I'm one of them. Other women completely break down. It is very demanding--lies, secrecy, being outed.

--My past was anything but glamorous. I've worked in penthouse apartments, right down to what can be described as chicken coops. I've been through tough times. Some days I absolutely adore my job. Some days I could cheerfully dangle my client by the ankles out the window.

CUCK

The largest pornography site in the world, PORNHUB, just released its annual Year in Review for 2018, which revealed that there's been an exponential increase in the number of users searching for **Cuckold-in-Chains** sex.

ENEMA

Word on e-Street is that cock jocks hold "gay try-outs" by inviting a manly man over to play the red wine-up-your-ass game.

With our e-version, you'll be flat on your ass in minutes.

Please do your research and know your limits!

Available in black rubber or clear silicone.

MILK MASSAGE

Client strips, lies tummy-down on the table.

Nude masseuse massages his back & ass & legs.

She may or may not insert a finger in his ass to stroke his prostate.

Depends how much he pays up front.

She removes a towel in the center of the table exposing a hole.

He sticks his cock & balls through the hole.

Like the gloryhole except cock pointing south.

The masseuse slips under the massage table and proceeds to "milk" his cock and balls while stroking her pussy.

Impersonal, n'est-ce-pas?

That's the turn-on.

They cum simultaneously.

More or less.

BLACK WHITE

White dick size larger than 5-and-a-half inches is rare. Black dick size smaller than 5-and-a-half-inches is scarcely possible.

White dick size may be smaller, but at least we form civil societies, have a much higher IQ, invent shit, and are able to enslave an entire race. We fucked over your folks for 500 years. Remember?

TOO BIG

We were shocked when we heard she cut her son's privates.

Neighbors said she called them screaming for help after severing the manhood which she described as *too big for his age*.

MANHOOD

The greatest trauma in a male's life afflicted YY when his penis was severed during a domestic violence dispute.

All that remained was about one centimeter of his former manhood.

Life was miserable for him physically and emotionally.

His sex life sucked.

He was having a hard time peeing.

On his knees he begged the surgeon to save him from the misery.

The surgeon, uncommonly empathic, agreed to perform the first penis transplant surgery in the country's long history.

The donated organ was from a 22-year-old man who died in a skateboard accident.

The surgery was successful.

After just three weeks of recovery YY and his wife returned to the hospital requesting the removal of the transplanted organ.

Reportedly, YY's wife, who'd severed YY's penis in the domestic dispute, could not tolerate another man's penis on her husband.

The same surgeon who performed the transplant severed YY's penis a second time.

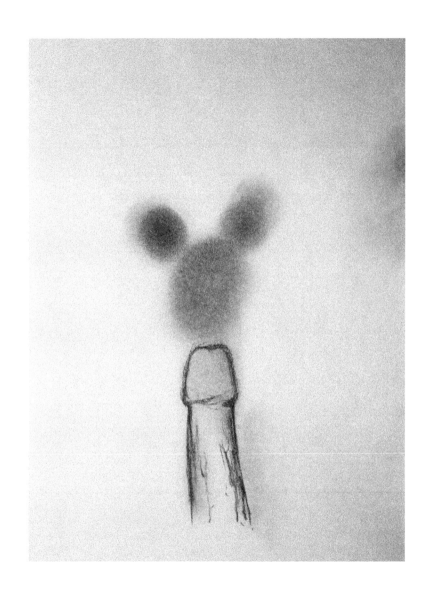

TOILET SLAVE

Will make full use of the shitter.

Flush or squat shitter, your pref.

Flush has more options.

Squat is closer to the action, more degrading, which is kool.

Ready water in the flusher is better for drowning.

Porn waterboarding.

Try it, don't diss it.

Poop disappears in the flusher, which is both sexy & not.

With the pulsing, striated asshole gone viral, poop is what you adore.

What our post-millennial *mise-en-scene* demands.

You know that Disney has a mega-stake in online porn, right?

When asked to explain, the Disney exec said simply:

People would rather stay home & masturbate than go out to a family movie.

TOILET SLAVE

As soon as I saw you I said to myself: Perfect!

You talk to yourself?

Yes.

Why would I be perfect?

Your shy eyes.
How you lick your lips.
The brown and gray designer stubble on your chops.
That tiny gap between your top front teeth.

I've never been a toilet slave before.

You're a pale male and you're cherry.
That's what we're looking for.

I'm not sure I'll like it.

You haven't tried it.

How many will do me?
Will they be female?

Depends on how many you can take.
Females and trans-folk will do you.

What about the pay?

What about it?

How much will I earn?

More than you earned at Burger King.

Can I think about it?

No.

(Pause)

Okay.
I'll give it a shot.
When do we begin?

Right now.
Everything's in place.
Hop into my purple Beemer.

NORWEGIAN CAR DRAMA

A male faces a hefty fine and driving ban after being caught having oral sex with his girlfriend while speeding on a motorway in Norway.

Officers initially trailed the couple's yellow Fiat after noticing it was swerving from side to side and traveling at 30 mph over the road's speed limit.

They soon realized the erratic driving was due to a nude female "straddling the male's head."

How did she manage the balancing act?
And in a tiny yellow, Italian-made Fiat?

Police said the 26-year-old driver was likely to face a fine of several thousand kroner and a lengthy driving ban.

Despite her prominent role in the incident, the 22-year-old acrobatic female was permitted by police to drive her sex-partner home.

POCKET MAN

was arrested in a Copenhagen mall and charged with 700 sexual assaults on young boys.

Danish media dubbed the suspect "Pocket Man" because he didn't wear underpants and kept a hole in his trouser pocket.

Boys were "assaulted" when lured to stick their hand into his trouser pocket.

FLUSH

The murderer "did his business but didn't flush," said Detective Tim of the Ventura Police. Result: DNA evidence led to the arrest of Tat for the murder of Tsiao.

Tat's indiscretion allowed investigators to collect evidence to conduct a DNA profile which matched another profile in a national database; detectives tracked down the suspect at his home in the city of Ventura.

Detective Tim said it was the first DNA murder case he knew of involving evidence collected from a toilet.

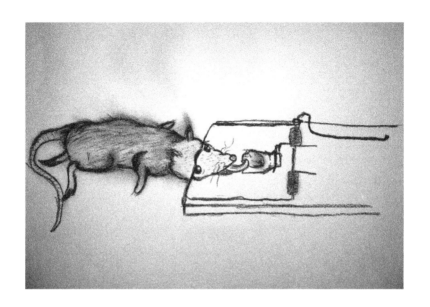

RATS

The ubiquitous, often diseased, Brown Rat (*Rattus norvegicus*) will emerge in toilet bowls after crawling through sewer pipes, and bite, even sever, humans' genitals.

Sensitive males, who now pee sitting down so as not to spray on the toilet seat and floor, face a dilemma. Do they follow the "politically correct" counsel and pee like a female, with the prospect of having their genitals severed? Or do they assert their old-school malehood and pee standing up, spraying wayward pee hither and yon?

SIZE

You're rather small down there. If you don't mind my saying.

It's not size it's how you use it.

How **do** you use it?

You know the phrase polymorphous perversity?

Wilhelm Reich?

No. The master. Sigmund Freud. Polymorphous perversity. Making love as children do.

Children?

The entire body equally privileged. I remember an image from the Sixties of two counter-culture teens, male and female, walking away from the camera in each other's arms. Their long hair, beads, and loose jeans--you couldn't tell female from male. That's how I make love.

That's how you use that tiny pilot down there.

Absolutely.

GOOD PORN

Has porn had a positive impact on sex?

Porn and erotic media provide sexual stimulus and fantasy for consumers.

Porn gives people who may have undeveloped social, physical, or emotional abilities access to sexual stimulation.

Porn gives people in geographically limited and socially challenged communities access to sex that may be "controversial" or stigmatized in their immediate surroundings.

Porn gives performers and models and producers the opportunity to explore their own sexualities.

Porn grants business people permission to get creative with products and marketing contra the stigma and limitations placed on erotic media from mainstream culture.

IgA

Having sex once or twice a week has been found to raise your body's levels of an antibody called immuno-globulin-A or IgA, which protects you from viral and bacterial infections. People who have sex more than once a week had 30% higher levels of IgA than those who abstained.

During sex, the natural steroid DHEA is secreted throughout the body and after an orgasm the level in the bloodstream soars to five times its normal amount. Known as the anti-ageing hormone, high levels of DHEA keep your body fitter and disease-free, helping you to live longer.

An Australian study found that people who had an orgasm at least three times a week had a 51% lower chance of dying from any medical reason than those who only climaxed once a month.

SEX MYTHS DEMYSTIFIED

Myth: You can't get diseases though oral sex.

Fact: Wrong. You can contract gonorrhea, chlamydia, syphilis, HPV and herpes simplex virus from any oral-genital contact.

Myth: If you feel fine, you're fine.

Fact: Wrong. Most STDs are asymptomatic. The only way to know if you have them is to get tested.

Myth: You'll know if your sexual partner has an STD by looking at them.

Fact: Wrong.

Myth: You can get STDs from toilet seats.

Fact: Wrong. But it will help if you do your due diligence and wipe the toilet seat before use with an FDA-approved antiseptic.

Myth: If you only have sex with someone once you're probably fine.

Fact: Wrong. Any kind of sexual contact with someone, even if it's only once, can get you infected.

Myth: It doesn't matter what kind of sex you're having—if it's protected, no problem.

Fact: Wrong. Sexual contact involving any kind of abrasion--from a canker to a cut--increases the likelihood of transmission with or without "protection."

Myth: Getting an STD once means you're immune later.

Fact: Wrong. Certain strains of chlamydia may confer a degree of protection from re-infection, but for syphilis, gonorrhea, genital warts, and hepatitis you can get infected again and again.

Myth: If you're not having sex with a new person every night, you don't need to get tested.

Fact: Wrong. You should get tested between sexual partners, right after getting a new partner, and once every two to four months if you're having sex with multiple people over that period. If you're in a long-term, monogamous relationship, you should get tested whenever you get regular physicals.

Myth: Sex can still be fun and not anxiety producing.

Fact: Wrong. Unless you are performing on an online porno site secretly governed by Disney, Goog, Verizon, Amazon . . .

AMERIPORN

I reckon you heard

Americans are great again, every orifice in biz

When 2 or 3 hetero dudes do a fem--up, down, upside-down--cocks pound near each other but don't never touch

Code, dude

This ain't the boy scouts

Swingin dick

You heard of Texas

We ain't seceded yet

AmeriPorn's a Texas thang

Big-big dollar shot & creamy pearl necklace

SILICONE

We passed a couple of these out to our employees and boys as samples. The verdict was unanimous. This is one of the most amazing everyday cockrings we've worn. In fact, most of the guys around the shop are wearing one now. Made from 100% silicone, the Super Soft Cockring stretches to go on easy and stays tight once it's on. It has a flat band so it won't roll down and pull your pubes like round rubber rings. It is safe for all the lube, spit, cum and piss you're going to smear on it. It stands up to whatever you choose to clean it with--if you choose to clean it.

BLACK SITE

Abu Zubaydah wearing filthy diapers crawls into the small confinement box without protest.

Abu Zubaydah is moved back and forth between the large and small confinement boxes and repeatedly slammed against a wall, an interrogation technique known as "walling."

Abu Zubaydah in his filthy diapers is informed again that he could end the torment if he tells interrogators what they want to know.

The waterboard is rolled in.

Abu Zubaydah in his filthy diapers remains silent.

Abu Zubaydah is broken during the three-week "aggressive phase" of interrogation.

Abu Zubaydah is rendered "utterly compliant," then dies.

Abu Zubaydah's interment sequence should be used as a default template for future interrogation of high value captives.

BURIED ALIVE

According to a 2004 CIA Interrogation with Extreme
Prejudice (IEP) memo, a high-value detainee (HVD)
can be bound in contorted stress positions, subjected
to deafening noise, sleep deprived to the point of
hallucination, deprived of food, drink, and medical care,
waterboarded, sexually taunted and humiliated,
subjected to extreme heat or extreme cold, confined
in small coffin-like boxes, repeatedly slapped, and
"walled" once (one violent impact with the wall) to 30
times when the interrogator requires a more "substantial"
response to a question.

Certain official restraints *were* imposed.
For example, the Justice Department narrowly rejected
a CIA proposal to bury detainees alive.

MAX HARDCORE

Is synonymous with "Gonzo Porn," loosely adapted from Hunter Thompson's "gonzo journalism," where zero distance is established between events & the recording of those events.

Max Hardcore (born Paul Little, in Wisconsin), is himself director, often photographer & main actor—a slightly built balding man with a small but erect penis & satanic grin, who wears a white cowboy hat while violently sodomizing, peeing, fisting, or otherwise sexually abusing a faux-teen or adolescent (actresses must be 18-years-old), usually Latina or Asian, poor-seeming, seized from the mean streets. So that the fantasy of brutal rape for $$ is always suggested.

Max Hardcore served two years & change in federal prison for forced sex with underage participants. That the participants were over the age of 18 was not disputed; the charges were based on the fact that Max Hardcore actresses were *portraying* underage characters.

Max reportedly commented: *If I'm serving two years, Disney. Exxon & the other shadow corporations that own the fuckin porn industry, should be doing two lifetimes.*

MOOCH

One thing that's really cool is chaining my sub for a couple hours while I tend to other things: go to the gym, the Apple store, Trader Joe's. While I'm out and about I enjoy thinking of how pissed he is, how he's cussing me out. What can I say, I'm a bastard at heart. Then I go home and fuck him superhard. My sub used to hate this, but one day I bought him the Mooch cock-extender-buttplug combo.

Now I chain him, slip this on him. The extender keeps his cock long and hard, the buttplug gets him horny as fuck, and when I get home he's eager to play. The Mooch is a great investment.

THAI PORN

Thailand's large prostitution population in big cities &
beaches slip-slides into the algorithmic grid, with **Street
Meat**, **Thai Hooker,** and **Bar Girl** as online rubrics
(opposed, for example, to a Japanese porn sequence
called **Schoolgirl's Pretty Panties**).

The Japanese teen is a sweet slut.
The Thai teen is a slut-slut.

Thai porn fem does online what she does in her offline
sexspace, more stylized online, a tech directs her
twerkings for the global audience.
Her sex-partners are black, white, well-endowed.
Thai males are too thin & small for prime time.
Thai males are just right for trans girly-boy sites.
Thai fems are more impassive online than off.
Impassive is the turn-on.

The more cultivated Thai sex involving intergender
humans & campy gay humor is a hit in Thai clubs, but
no invite online for global viewers.
How come?
Cuz the "fems" ain't impassive. And they ain't that sexy
either.

FILIPINA PORN

Not Thai?

American male porn surfers can't tell the difference

Slender Asian street girls with tats

Thai porn girls are taller

They wear very high heels

Filipina porn girls are less impassive

Colonialist Spain in their blood

They could also be faking it

Filipina porn girls pole-dance naked

Filipina porn girls rarely sex with Filipino males who tend to be small all over

They sex with BBCs & white American males

Alone / ensemble

Each male is hung a mile

BRAZIL PORN

is relaxed

Skin tones range from blonde to ebony

Everyone is sexy & supple

Everyone has tats

Brazilian Portuguese sounds samba lovely on the
tongue

The actors appear to like each other

Resembles Sixties sex

Age of Aquarius

Sexy but not erotic which means not pornographic

Cruelty & death must occupy a privileged space for sex
to be porn that creeps & zooms

Brazil porn ain't that

DUTCH PORN

Like Danish porn years before, was well ahead of the curve until becoming paranoid about Muslim refugee terrorists, turned to the Right, cut off hash, open sex, clean needles for heroin addicts, and sounded like Apartheid South Africans.

You can hear the Afrikaans cadences in their talk.

In a country-wide poll a racist, Muslim-hating, right-wing film-maker freshly assassinated, who (hideous irony) was named after Theo Van Gogh, his great-grandfather and loving brother of Vincent, easily outdistanced Rembrandt, Vermeer and Vincent as the most admired Dutch artist ever.

Dutch bigs devoutly consider turning the Red Light district into a 24-7 shopping mall.

EBONY PORN

Has nothing to do with black fems except maybe their booties.

Hung black men are primo, referred to as BBC.

Big Black Cock.

Virtually always in biracial company, often with "petite" girl partners.

The brothers--some of them--recognize they are being used for their bodies, not unlike the slaveholders who sipped juleps and watched their naked slaves wrestle.

But these bros are young and virile which means they can fuck "exotic" fems and make a few $$.

First things first.

PAWG

Phat Ass White Girl.

Black male "urban" slang.

Twerks her phat ass.

Twerks her phat ass while blowing a monster BBC.

Twerks her phat ass while getting brutally fucked.

Twerks her phat ass while getting brutally fucked in her phat ass.

Teenaged phat ass white girl, awesome.

Does she have the coveted thigh gap as well?

You're asking for too much. **Repeat**:

She's an awesome teen phat ass white girl, Hallelujah.

She's an awesome teen phat ass white girl, Hallelujah.

ROCCO

Porn super-stud "Italian Stallion" legend Rocco Siffredi puts it this way: "I want to see emotion, fear, female eyes shooting skyward in erotic astonishment."

He's gone by different names but will always be known to any fem who fucked & sucked with him as the stud who transported them to limits they never envisioned.

In our moral panic as the warring world wanes, Rocco's porn vids have the capacity to transport the whole globe, including versatile Satan, into a mega-collective orgy.

He directs his flix as if his massive cock were an enchanted paintbrush on an enormous canvas covered in sweat, squirt & cum.

Slapping, choking, spitting, pissing, smothering— Rocco loves to give as much as he loves to get, so everyone is immensely, deliriously fucked up in the end.

One category where the Italian Stallion excels is ultimate anal domination. Rocco makes buttholes wink & blink before he even reaches for his fly, then, mad minutes later, presents them or her wit a creampie so dat busted-up ass be tastin' like birthday cake.

Rocco is emperor in an industry filled with pole-jousting stunt-dicks. One look at his scenes & you've entered a kingdom where every fuck freak is sure to freak out utterly.

Rocco's an AVN Hall-of-Famer with 66 major awards under his jocks.

JAPAN PORN

Is the most creatively inclusive on the Net.
Note the "contradictions," such as the convention of the
girl or woman making a desperate "I am being raped"
face whining loudly in mortal pain.
At the same time deliriously contributing to the "brutal"
sex at hand.

Hegel would call the transaction **Aufheben**:
simultaneous pull/push.

*The push simulation is designed to sell—Young women
raped.*
*The pull endorsement is designed to sell—Young
women squirt in ecstasy.*

JAPAN PORN

Physical passion in public is firmly discouraged.
Online every function is sexualized.
Spit, fart, pee, poop, vomit, menstruate . . .
Fetish keenly, wackily inventive.
[Blood and snuff available but strictly VIP (yen yen)]
A porn skit may contain numerous actors--a dozen
semi-naked girls and a single male.
The girls giggling, scrutinizing the single girl in action.
[Japanese tourists with their cameras]

Unlike AmeriPorn where participants are enhanced,
tattooed, naked, Japanese slip in and out of clothing,
lingerie, peek-a-boo.

Females are breasty, cuddly, often bowlegged, just as
often surprisingly long-legged.
Males, with few exceptions, are under-endowed, hence
not foregrounded.
They are enslaved, peed, shat on.

The schizoid Japanese law commands that all genitals,
excluding the anus, male and female, be pixelated,
obscured.

[Advanced porn sites penetrate the pixels (yen yen)]

CUDDLE CAFE

The first Soine-ya, or "nap together shop," opened last year in Tokyo, permitting male customers to nap next to a clothed young girl for a fee.

Sexual requests are prohibited.

GAMESHOW

She is young, lovely, dressed with a low-key elegance.
Eminently serious.

6 o'clock.

She is the Japanese TV anchor here to deliver the
news.

The first male in a beige poplin suit approaches from
her left, unzips his fly and sprays her hair and the top of
her face.

She continues reciting the news.

The second male in a black and grey seersucker sport
jacket approaches her from her right, unzips his fly and
ejaculates on her cheek and chin.

She continues to recite the news.

Two males from either side approach unzip their flies
and drip sperm on her nose and mouth.

She wipes her mouth with a tissue and continues to
recite the news.

Multiple males come from left and right and ejaculate
on her face and in her hair.

Briefly she wipes her face and continues to recite the
news.

The news is favorable.

Today is a good day.

COSPLAY

Love-struck fans across Japan have expressed dismay about reports that the exceptionally cute girl they adore is a boy.

The reports referred to online sites which provided "proof" that the cosplayer who went by the name of TAK is a male.

But knowing fans have since pointed out that TAK has been plagued by those rumors because she has an oversized clitoris that can be mistaken for a penis.

In truth, TAK is every bit as female as she looks, and the news sources have since apologized to her love-struck fans for unintentionally disseminating inaccurate information.

MILK ENEMA

Japan murders dolphins and whales but adores stuffed animals.

In a small gym-like setting a svelte Japanese Dom in a black PVC "catsuit" administers milk enemas to six kneeling naked ass-spread teenaged girls.

The girls' anuses are front and center, but their vaginas are obscured by "mosaics" in accord with an ancient Japanese censorship edict.

The girls look straight ahead blankly.

The Dom uses an elegant suction tube which she fills with milk several times for each girl's enema.

The girls are then divided into three pairs.

Each pair, naked, asses filled with milk, wrestles on individual mats.

The loser of each match is then compelled to bathe in and drink the milky fluid the victor sprays from her asshole.

The Dom makes her rounds to assure that her edicts
are obeyed.

Then she orders the wrestling losers to kneel and spray
milk from their assholes which she—svelte Dom in
black PVC catsuit—swallows with gusto.

PEEING N POOPING

are an inescapable part of being human; so is being embarrassed. Many humans dread letting loose in a public restroom or, even worse, in the bathroom of a small house with family and friends quietly sitting in an adjoining room. What are they to do?

Thanks to Japanese ingenuity, they can use the palm-sized pee-n-poop audio masker, code-named Keitai Otohime.

Japan's first attempt to mask the unpleasant sounds of defecation was the Otokeshi-no Tsubo ("Urn for Covering the Sound") at the turn of the 20th century. Currently it resides at the Takage Folk Museum in Okayama Prefecture.

Next was the 1988 Otohime (which means "sound princess"), an electronic "jukebox" that produces an audio flush via the push of a button. It's still popular today and can be found in department stores and office buildings across Japan.

Fast-forward two decades and behold Keitai Otohime. The revolutionary portable device you can interface to your smartphone. It masks the sounds of pee-n-poop by reproducing 1 of 70 "tunes," varying from the silken zen swoosh of bamboo to John Lennon singing "Imagine."

Released in November 2009 by Takara Tomy Arts, the Keitai Otohime--priced at ¥1,449, or approximately $14.99--relies on two AAA batteries to deliver 611 flushes, which for the average pooper means good for half a year.

SNAGGLE

Japanese adolescent and teen girls have become obsessed with uneven or "snaggle" teeth, known in Japanese as "yaeba," and thought to be sexy.

The pic below is a before-and-after of a newly "yaeba'd" young girl with a smile on her snaggle teeth as she leaves her dentist's office.

FOREVER ALONE

Humans may become past tense thanks to a new Japanese-created device that hugs you back.
Called SenseRoid, it is essentially a virtual hug in the form of a mannequin.
Developed by researchers at the University of Electro-Communications, the device won the overall prize at IVRC 2014.

Using vibration motors, tactile sensors, and artificial muscles, the device allows the user to hug it and receive a "virtual hug" in exchange.
The device doesn't have arms, as such, so it doesn't *actually* hug you back, but it will make the user feel like they're hugging themselves.

When humans embrace they receive a nice feeling of security and satisfaction.
Along those lines, we wondered how people would feel if they could hug themselves, the person with whom they have the closest relationship, and so we created this.

KOREAN PORN

Has devolved into a footnote to Japanese, Thai,

Philippine, Chinese porn.

Females are pretty, males are firm.

You won't find pixelated genitals.

If energy is eternal delight, South Korea presents us

misery.

I'm overstating.

25 years ago Korea was a major player.

Now Korean porn is neutral.

No tats.

Could there be other ways to have devil-fun for nice

money?

If so, please text me asap.

BRITISH PORN

Goonshow works best.

One sequence called **Fake Taxi** has a London "cabbie"

seduce his female passenger in the back seat.

"Hallo, Luv, hop right in."

The passengers are foreigners in London.

Occasionally a passenger is British.

She is doughy & tattooed.

Like the Germans they despise, Brit porn favors Bukkake.

The 10 masturbating males don't have six-pack abs.

Their sperm sprays but mostly drips.

The fem swallows what doesn't miss the mark.

Swallow is *de rigueur.*

Messy biz.

Fish n chips with too much vinegar & no nappie.

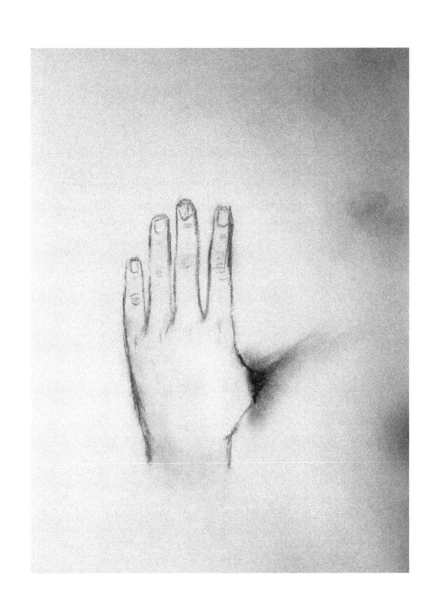

.

4 FINGERS

A new bill would ban sex acts from UK porn.

The Digital Economy Bill (DEB) wants to ban anything that wouldn't be permitted on a commercially available DVD. That would severely limit adult content, ban viewer-pleasing acts like female squirting, whipped cream enemas, machine sex, face sitting, golden showers, monstercocks, even menstrual blood.

While there are no strict guidelines as to what acts and images are restricted on commercial DVDs, adult film producers have had to cut all manner of non-conventional sequences from their videos.

Such restrictions include the "4-finger rule," which limits the number of digits that can be inserted into any orifice while on vid.

Irrespective of digit size?

Irrespective. Yes.

TONGUE

A Tyneside woman deliberately bit her boyfriend's tongue during a drunken birthday kiss.

Gillian Cox, 40, bit a third of Nigel Foxell's tongue off and appeared to swallow it.

They were celebrating Nigel Foxell's 46th birthday at his bedsit when she grew upset that he had not made her pregnant.

Nigel Foxell explained that he was too busy visiting online porno sites to worry about pregnancy.

It was then that Gillian Cox bit a third of Nigel Foxell's tongue off and appeared to swallow it.

DARKWEB

A British model was kidnapped and held captive in Italy for six days by a Polish national who reportedly intended to auction her on the dark web.

The Polish male has been arrested on suspicion of kidnapping for extortion purposes after the 20-year-old woman was returned to the British consulate in Milan.

The woman who had come to Milan for a photoshoot was abducted on 11 July. She was drugged and transported in a bag to Borgial, an isolated village near Turin.

The Polish male tried to sell the woman online for £230,000 but was unsuccessful when it was discovered the model had a young child thus was unsuitable for sex trafficking.

She was kept handcuffed to furniture but freed after six days and removed to the British embassy in Milan.

The abductor is still at large.

STREAKER

He danced and pranced, somersaulted over the net and curtsied to the crowd. For the second time in 3 years, the men's final at Wimbledon was interrupted by a naked prankster cavorting on Centre Court.

The 36-year-old pale male--a self-described "serial streaker"--enlivened the proceedings during a rain break in Djokovic's straight-set mauling of Andy Murray. The male leaped onto the court, shed his clothes, kicked off his shoes and performed a little jig at the net. As spectators laughed and cheered, he did a pirouette, curtsied, flipped over the net and flexed his biceps.

The streaker evaded two male guards, before he was tackled by a female guard (a rugger, originally from New Zealand, recently transitioned from M2F), and escorted away with an orange sheet around him.

Portions of the incident were shown live on BBC-TV, which screened full-frontal footage of the man before cutting away. NBC showed most of the episode to its U.S. audience but with strategically placed blurring.

The streaker, identified as Graham Swinburne, of East Anglia, claimed 155-and-a-half streaking "performances" during an eight-year run. He was remanded to Wimbledon police station for questioning.

Sunday's incident was the second Centre Court security breach this year. During the first week, two naked males carrying rackets eluded security and hit a ball back and forth for about 20 seconds.
They calmly exited the complex without being apprehended.

All England Club spokes-human Basil Lounder said in a statement that "Security has been reviewed, and it is a difficult compromise between containment and the splendid views and proximity to the court that spectators enjoy at Wimbledon."
The larger question still obtains:

Why is streaking so much more prevalent in perishing England than elsewhere in the civilized world?

Is it the entrenched British Monty Python sensibility?

Is it because old England is fading fast and needs any entertainment it can muster?

Is it simply because Brits like to display their pale bodies on those rare days when the British skies don't moodily piss?

GOBSMACKED

Australian victims of faulty pelvic mesh implants have expressed disgust at doctors' suggestions of sodomy as a solution to their ruined sex lives.

A disturbing email exchange between doctors emerged earlier this month as part of a federal court class action in Australia launched by hundreds of women who had the devices implanted to treat childbirth complications.

The devices, manufactured by pharmaceutical giant Johnson & Johnson, caused chronic, debilitating pain during intercourse.

The email exchanges reflected a callous attitude towards women especially among French gynecologists involved with the company. "Sodomy may be the most viable alternative!" one wrote. Several gynecologists concurred.

The comments outraged members of the Australian Pelvic Mesh Support Group, which presented a collection of anonymous responses from women who encountered similar attitudes from their own physicians.

"My husband and I were given advice about sexual activity," one said. "We were gobsmacked. The suggestion that women who are unable to have vaginal intercourse should practice anal instead completely devalues a woman's right to a full and healthy sex life as an active, empowered and fulfilled participant."

GERMAN PORN

We regret to say, is aggressive, violent

There are numerous German "Bukkake" and piss sites

Messy action

The woman swallowing is handled roughly

Which she loves

German producers are providing the massive

international online porn audience with something

they think we'll think is primo Hun

And will purchase

The scenes themselves are acted, not inhabited

Then again, what the German industrialists' porn actors

sell may represent what they *actually are* in and out of

porn

We are in 2019 / Where is the out of porn?

RUSSIAN PORN

Dissolution of the Soviet Union / floodgates fling open.
Russia is all over sex & sex that sells.
Russian fems are sexy & gorgeous.
Russian males are muscled & hung.

Slip into online hardline porn?
No prob.
Fems are risky & funky.
Males don't give a shit.
That open attitude has always been part of Russia.
Repressed by the Tsar than the Communists.
So we're told.

CZECH PORN

First the Nazis

Then the Soviets

Then sudden manic Capitalism

Then Slovakia secedes

What next?

Pornography online, *bien sur*

Lewd gorgeous females with tats

Czechs eager for any (virtually any) extremity that pays

dividends for their secret sultriness and long suffering

FRENCH PORN

Has not fully joined the online global charade.

Here and there vids featuring French Eurasian fems.

Occasionally a black *grand-homme* from French-

colonized North Africa.

France may think their ecstatic body too refined for

promiscuous mass consumption.

They may object to English being the porn industry's

lingua franca.

They may resent that their naked ecstatic body online

will not look different enough than the German.

Or even the doughy Brits.

We were looking forward to some *Guignol* porn.

Sadistic, stylish, acrobatic marionettes.

Whispering obscenely in the *langue* we love to eat.

The cyberporn globe is waiting for France to either poop or get off the pot.

Don't undervalue the bidet.

France will keep us waiting.

NUDE IN PARIS

Parisian nudists will finally have a space to take it all off--for the next few weeks at least--at a secluded zone in the Bois de Vincennes east of the city.

"The creation of an area in the Bois de Vincennes where naturism will be authorized is part of our open-minded vision of Parisian public space," pronounced the deputy mayor in charge of parks.

The site, considered an experiment, will be open from Thursday 31 August until 15 October, from 8 am-7.30 pm.

Signs will let park users know what's going on / coming off in the clearing near the park's bird reserve, spread over 79,000 square feet.

Officials vow that no voyeurism or exhibitionism will be tolerated to assure courtesy to those making the most of their natural state.

"It's a true joy, one more freedom for naturists," said the CEO of the Paris Naturists Association, who estimated that thousands of people in the region will want to take advantage of the site.

"It shows the city's broad-mindedness and it will help

change people's attitudes toward nudity, toward our values and our respect for nature," the CEO said, adding that he has been a practicing nudist for 23 years.

Parisians already have one public pool where they can swim in the buff three times a week, and across the country some 460 areas are reserved for naked enjoyment, including 155 campsites and 73 beaches.

More than 2.6 million people in France have made nudism a regular habit, according to the Paris Naturists Association.

HAROLD JAFFE

CAMBODIAN PORN

Though Cambodia was formerly a "protectorate" of
France, it was only toward the end of his life that the
artist Rodin visited impoverished Cambodia for the
first time.

He was captivated by the young females, whom he
sketched lovingly.

Rodin noted that there was a delicacy of beauty among
these females that the West has never before seen.

Poor as Cambodia is, the females are rarely seen on
official porn sites.

Unlike other Southeast Asians such as Thai,
Vietnamese, Philippine.

Not because Cambodian Buddhism forbids it.

Because Cambodians have not yet considered that
now nearly universal axiom: *Display yourself utterly
while making money.*

MALE ON LEASH

Fujian province.

Strangers stare as a woman in a blue dress and stiletto heels strides toward the city center.

Two paces behind her is a male crawling on hands and knees, a black leather dog collar around his neck.

He struggles to keep up as the woman tugs on the leash attached to the collar.

Waiting for the traffic light to change, she orders the male to "stay."'

Police arrive, command the woman to unleash the man.

He is dog, not man, she declares.

No longer leashed, dog-man continues to trail her, 2 paces behind, head bowed, on hands and knees.

HAROLD JAFFE

Public spectacles in China frequently include wives
assaulting husbands' "mistresses."
However, the public shaming of a male, especially in
such a fashion, is relatively uncommon.

150

JU-LONG

In most cultures a wedding is a time of great joy and change. For one mother in China, her son's recent wedding ticked just one of those boxes. When the 31-year-old son brought home his fiancée, his mother knew that change was in the reckoning. She was not especially joyful, though, because her future daughter-in-law was a robot built by her son.

Zheng Jiajia works as a robot designer and artificial intelligence programmer in the city of Hangzhou. He tried dating for the last six years. but grew frustrated that he could not find "the one."

As a result he did what any self-respecting robot designer would do--he combined technical skills and lonely heart to erect the perfect wife. He quit his job at Huawei, the international telecommunication firm, and directed his energy toward his new love, an AI robot named Ju-Long. As of this writing, Ju-Long understands

151

Chinese characters and images and can even say a
few words. However, she cannot yet walk, which means
that Zheng had to carry her to and from their wedding, a
simple ceremony, attended by family and a handful of
friends.

Ju-Long wore a black dress and, in accord with
tradition, a red scarf draped over her head. Eventually,
the 31-year-old plans to upgrade his robot bride so that
she can help with the necessary chores.

INDIA PORN

Self-confessed electronic utopian, Indian PM Modi,
envisions a "digital India."
The resident macaque monkeys have not complied;
twice they chewed through the fiber-optic cables strung
along the banks of the Ganges.

The next best option would be to join the global porn
network.
View Bollywood fatties (fat has always been a sign of
blessed wealth in India) having a fuck and suck.
Don't expect *Kamasutra* agility; agile Indians are low
caste Indians who are shut out.

What's labeled India porn is often Lebanese, Turkish,
Iranian, Mexican.
So long as the actors are round and dark and females
have the tilak in the center of their forehead.

TANTRA

What is tantric sex?

Tantric sex is an ancient Hindu practice that dates back 5,000 years.

Etymologically, "tantra" means the weaving and expansion of energy, and tantric couples enjoy a slow form of sex in order to have hyper-potent orgasms.

What are the benefits of tantric sex?

Tantric sex provides an inside-out experience of your body along with a deep understanding of the world in pain.

Tantric sex's main benefit is longer, more potent orgasms.

How long do tantric orgasms last?

Tantric sex lovers Sean and Sienna from Forked River, New Jersey say they climax for 18 hours on end.

154

Thanks to tantra, Sean and Sienna can orgasm simply from "sexting."

Watch Sean and Sienna tremble and moan in pleasure as they share an algorithmic embrace.

ARAB PORN

Is absent from the Net, though faked.

Dark complected females naked with prominent pubic

bushes, wearing head coverings and exclaiming

orgasmically with *Aggghs*! and *Ayyys*!

Outlandish exclamations which sound more or less

Arabic to Disney and other US producers of mega-

profitable porn sites.

According to the algorithms, the "Arabic" sites have

become wildly popular with porn surfers since the

widely reported ISIS atrocities.

INFIDELITY

A Qatar Airways plane has been forced to land midflight after a woman who used her sleeping husband's thumb impression to unlock his smartphone discovered he was unfaithful.

The couple and their child were flying to Bali for a holiday after boarding in Doha. After learning of his infidelity, the woman, an Iranian national, commenced to scream while repeatedly punching her husband's face and head.

The captain was forced to make an unscheduled stop in Chennai, India. The family were offloaded at Chennai airport and left for Bali on a Batik Air flight at 10.30pm.

Qatar Airways declined comment.

HAROLD JAFFE

SPIT

We're naked, sprawled on the mat.

Cough up saliva and mucus from your respiratory tract.

Spit in my mouth and I will cough up saliva and mucus

and spit in your mouth.

Swallow.

Spit in my mouth again, deeper, harder.

I will spit in your mouth again deeper, harder.

Swallow.

INSATIABLE

I have been in a relationship for nearly 10 months. I thought the sex was good for us both, but when we finish she tells me go shower. I wondered why. Finally, peeking out of the bathroom I knew--she masturbates. She has done it multiple times. She may be insatiable. What do I do?

Do nothing. Have your shower. Let her get on with it. Many women crave a second orgasm, especially if she was super-aroused during intercourse.

Maybe she doesn't want to bother you for that extra pleasuring, or she is afraid you would think her too demanding.

Women find clitorally focused orgasms they have during masturbation qualitatively different from what is experienced during lovemaking. Masturbation can produce a deeply satisfying orgasm without the anxiety that sometimes accompanies partner sex.

Sex with you could be fulfilling for her in ways that cannot be reproduced during masturbation, but she still may want that extra jolt. You call that "insatiable"; I would call her "sexually proficient" and you "lucky" that she is so aroused by you.

Bottom line: If you wish to participate beyond your established love-making pattern, ask what exactly she would like you to do for her after you have climaxed.

Follow orders--or be told to hit the shower.

AFTER THE REVOLUTION

MLF With Bad Nosejob Gets Huge Cum Facial 3 BJ/Cumshots Vids
Teen Slut Swallowing Globs Of Hot Nut Butter 4 Latina HD GIFS
Blonde & Jap Swap Ass Cum 3 Anal/Ass GIFS
Vintage Sex Vids & Big Hairy Bushes 3 Amateur Action Vids
Pee Lovin Chick Asks For Mo' 4 Piss Action HD Vids
Mex Babe Spreads Pink & Gets Meatstick 3 Hardcore HD GIFS
Kinky Shaved Chubber Whips Her Whip 6 SM HD Flix
Asian Tight Twat Swallows Quart Sized Beer Bottle 4 Fetish/Bizarre GIFS
I Like To Squirt Over Myself Then Get Shagged 4 Hardcore Pics
Czech Cougar Swallowing Three Dicks Frottage 3 HD GIFS
Thick Latina Pissed Then Boned 3 Hardcore Pics
MILF In Pantyhose Gets Phat Ass Stuffed & Face Jizzed 4 Mature
Ladies Vids
Big Mamma Wraps Her Boobs Round A Stiffy 6 BBW HD GIFS
Girl With Grool 5 HD Vids
Shaved Head Babe Takes Mandingo's Mega-Cock 4 Action Vids
Cougar Stalks Son's Pal & Fucks Him With Green Strapon 5
Hardcore Hot Flix
Hardcore Electrical Lesbo Bondage 6 Bondage/BDSM Pics
Dom Drills Fem Slaves Snatch 6 Bondage/BDSM HD GIFS
2 Young Cunts A'Cookin In The Kitchen 6 Fetish/Bizarre Flix
Texas Twins Dip Their Honeypots In Bubble Bath 2 HD Vids
Babe Tossing Her Stud's Salad 3 Fetish/Bizarre Flix
Samantha Slurps Every Last Drop Of Goo 4 Porn Stars GIFS
Sex-crazed Twins, Tiffany N Mynx, Cumswap, 4 HD Vids
Tiny Titted Carmen Takes Two Big Dicks In Pooper 3 Latina Pics
Sissy Cuck in Chains Views Wife Suck & Fuck Monster BBC 6
Amateur HD Flix
Fisting Hard A Shaved Wet Puss 4 Fetish/Bizarre Pics

HAROLD JAFFE

Slutty Granny Does Herself With Baseball Batsized Dildo 4 Mature Ladies GIFS
Twelve Dudes Jizz On Bluehaired Emo's Grill 3 Bukkake HD Vids
Cheating Wives Do It For $$ 4 Amateur Action Flix
Monster Black Cock Gives Pearl Necklace 3 Interracial Pics
Mature Brit Bitch Milks Mandingo's BBC 3 Interracial GIFS
Lesbo Threesome Chain Asshole Licking 4 Lesbian HD GIFS
College Babes Fucking Sex Machines 3 Young Ladies Flix
Hot N Heavy Shemale Sex 6 Trans Pics
Two Muscle Bears Eat Each Other's Ass 5 Gay HD Vids
Horny Tranny Pleasures Two Nerds 4 Trans Vids
Roughneck Inked Stud Jacks His Cock 6 Gay Vids
Hot Jap Teens White Cotton Panties Ripped Off & Dicked! 4 Asian Pics
Ebony Plump Rumps Getting Humped By Black Horsedick 8 Mature Ladies HD Flix
Innocent Game Of Truth Or Dare Turns Into Wild Sex Orgy 3 Amateur Pics
Redhead Housewife Takes Butt Plug In Her Ass N Hot Man Sausage In Her Twat 3 7Amateur HotHot Vids
Horny Fem Prof Sucks Off College Student After Class 4 Big Tits Pics
Phat Slut Tugs On Hard Cock Till She Gets Her Face Painted Jizz 3 Amateur Action HD Flix
Long Tongued Stranger Licks Grannys Snatch In Graveyard 4 Hardcore Pics
Phat MLF Boned Hard On Bar Stool 6 Mature Ladies GIFS
Cutie Daphaney Gets A Long Hard Bonin 4 hardcore Flix
Tiny Asian Girls Smoke Huge Cigars & Swallow Man Juice 4 Interracial HD Flix
Sexy Fems Bound & Shocked To Orgasm 6 Bondage/BDSM Pics
Uh-Oh A Dominatrix In Rubber With An 18 Inch Strap-On 6 BDSM HD Flix

Chick In Chains Gets Her Snatch Stretched 6 Fetish/Bizarre Flix
3 Naked Young Babes Play With Mud 4 Young Ladies GIFS
Tranny Porks Her Eager Boyfriend 6 Trans Flix
Brunette & Redhead Trade Anal Creampie 5 Anal/Ass Flix
Wifey With Huge Melons Facialized 3 Big Tits Pics
Skinny Goth Does Gloryhole In Raunchy Loo 2 BJ/Big Cum HD Vids
Kristina Flashes Her Fake Boobs In Convenience Store 4 Big Tits Pics
Asian Eager Beaver Balling Huge White Dick 9 Asian Action Flix
Anime Hardcore Action 6 Anime GIFS
Lesbos Caught With Sextoy In Public Mens Toilet 6 Lesbian Pics
Milf And Shaved Head Daughter Share A BBC 3 Hardcore Hot Action Flix
Hunky Amateur Stroking 5 Gay HD Flix
Hot Pigtail Pisses Boyfriend 3 Hardcore Pics
White Boys Work Over Busty Nubian 3 Interracial GIFS
Two Dirty Moms Slobber Down Big Black Cock 5 Mature Ladies Pics
Nice Nanny Gets Rammed In The Browneye 5 Hardcore Vids
Wrinkly Phat Granny Drilled On Barstool 3 Mature Ladies Pics
Three Girls Have Some Clit Lickin Fun 3 Lesbian HD Vids
Slant Eye for the Straight Guy 3 Action Flix
Tiny Little Ripe Rump Slathered In Cream 3 Young Ladies Pics
Indian Chick Swallowing Three Studs Creamy Curry 4 Asian HD Vids
Twink & Bear In Raunchy Suck N Fuck 6 Gay HD Flix
Sperm Spitting Bukkake Fetish Panic 4 Japanese Pics
Wacko Bitch Uses Speculum To Cum Bigtime 5 Fetish/Bizarre GIFS
Euro MMF Cumshot Extravaganza 3 Group HotHot Vids
Hot Redhead Gets Nasty Rimjob 3 Anal And Ass Vids
Mature Street Skank Plays Suck N Tell 3 Hardcore Pics
Hot Booty Blonde In 9-Inch Heels Ass Boned Hard 3 Anal/Ass HD GIFS
Watch Her Cum Right in Yo Face 3 Pussy Closeups HD GIFS
Chubby Using Toes To Diddle Hard Cock To Cum 4 BBW Flix
Anal Booty Winking 3 Asshole Closeups HD GIFS
Asian Squatting & Peeing 4 Fetish/Bizarre Pics

Messy German Milk Enemas 5 Fetish/Bizarre Pics
Electro Torment In The Funk Garage 6 Bondage/BDSM Pics
Big Breasted Jane In Tittie Torments 6 Bondage/BDSM HD Vids
Spunktastic Cockgobblers Go Public In Stripmall 6 HD Flix
Fem Wrestler Gets Cameltoe Puss Licked 6 Lesbian Pics
High School Hotshot Bones Bubble Booty Cheerleader 5 Hardcore GIFS
Petite Lisa Loves Black Ghetto Cock 3 Interracial HD Flix
Crazy voyeur Creaming On Sleeping Girl Boobs 5 Voyeur Vids
Anime Rides Cock And Gets Facejizzed 4 Anime Pics
Hentai Girl Getting Pussy Hammered 4 Anime Pics
Zitty Babe Rides The Sybian 4 Amateur Action Flix
Chick Attempts To Swallow Monster Dong 3 BJ Cumshots Pics
Goth Babe Gets Ass Slammed N Gaped 4 Anal/Ass Pics
Tiny Dick Sissies Watch Wives With Big Cock Strangers 3
Bondage/BDSM Flix
PAWG Teen Gets It In The Booty From Her Stepbro 5 Anal/Ass HD GIFS
Lady Sonia Ass-Smothering 5 Bondage/BDSM Vids
Young Cutie Gets Double Dicked 7 Anal/Ass HD Flix
Blonde Mature In Hardcore Threesome 4 Cougar HD Vids
Cumaholic Babe Doing Deepthroat 5 Fetish/Bizarre HD Vids
3 Jap Chicks Assboned & Creamed 4 Group Pics
Skinny Alt Babe Rough Fuck N Creampie 3 HD Flix
3 Horny Dudes Fucking Fleshlights 3 HD Vids
Lola Sucks A Priests Holy Cock 3 Porn Stars Pics GIFS
Facialing Two Cum Thirsty Cuties 4 BJ/Cumshots Pics
Petite Blonde Sucking Balls N Ass 4 Anal And Ass Pics
Oh No! Cockzilla! 6 Crazycock HD Vids

WEIMAR

No authoritarian government will permit "pornography."

Except at the highest level.

The billion dollar porn industry will be assaulted by official lies:

There's a new venereal disease that doesn't readily show up in blood. Its consequences are worse than AIDS.

Repression, such as what happened after Weimar, will descend upon the land.

ADDICTION

A male has revealed how he accumulated 18 terabytes of porn on his computer then took the heroic step of deleting it all to help him overcome his addiction.

A terabyte is 1,000 gigabytes, so the male's 18 terabyte collection is equivalent to 5,400 hours of high quality video or 64.8 million images. At a rate of watching eight hours of video per day, it would have taken him 20 months of daily viewing to get through his entire collection.

"I would get a rush downloading all I could, spending days at a time just downloading vid after vid, even creating lightweight PHP bots to do it," the male wrote on a Reddit forum dedicated to humans unhooking themselves from pornn.

Experts were shocked by how big the male's porn collection was, but everyone congratulated him on getting rid of it.

18 terabytes of poison, the recovering porn addict wrote on his blog.

18 terabytes of self-deception, eluding yourself, deceiving your brain.

18 terabytes of social awkwardness, lack of confidence, fear in the heart.

18 terabytes of a fake, digital relationships with paid performers on screen.

18 terabytes of wiring your brain into a dopamine-overloaded junkyard.

SEXUAL ADVICE TO ELDERS

Contrary to belief, sexual desire is one of the last functions elders lose in their golden years, so tag-teaming with PORNHUB to teach elders valuable lessons on how to have safe-sex is a no-brainer.

With this video we hope to give our parents and grand-parents bedroom advice to decrease the spread of disease and injuries when playing helicopter with Mr. Johnson.

The main issue is that many seniors think contraception only prevents pregnancy. Thus, they are forgoing condoms, causing a spike in venereal diseases, which can be especially dangerous for decrepit humans with weak immune systems.

To help stop the spreading of STDs among parents, grandparents and great-grandparents, without whom we would not be here today, we created this sex-ed video, old school style, and we made it available both on VHS and online, so no matter how electronically inept an elder is, they can access the video.

"Old School" is produced by PORNHUB'S philanthropic arm.

ЯR

Fe

HAROLD JAFFE

BB & MM

Countries respond to each other unequally.

The UK has France on its mind, both admiring and despising them.

France does not have the UK on its mind.

France has the US on its mind, both admiring and scoffing at them.

The US doesn't bother with the French.

France knows everything about Marilyn Monroe—her working-class background, her husbands and lovers, her movies, her suicide attempts. The French admire MM, if slightly condescendingly.

The US knows almost nothing about Marilyn Monroe's Gallic counterpart, Brigitte Bardot—her upper-middle-class background and racist family, her multiple marriages and affairs, her professed love for animals and open loathing of Muslims.

MM remained tragic and died young. She looked spectacular dead.

BB is old, alive, hyper-rich, a breast-cancer survivor, adoring animals and loathing immigrants.

Certain ugliness can be appealing.

WC Fields. Harpo Marx. Margaret Rutherford.

Stephen Hawking.

Not BB.

She has become cruelly, dishearteningly ugly.

GOD DID IT

A 42-year-old homeless man believed to be linked to two feces attacks is in custody.

Two women in separate incidents had feces violently shoved down their pants.

Police said they believed a homeless person was behind this week's attacks and that the women did not know their attacker.

The man, discovered in a junkyard in downtown Brooklyn, was identified as XX, homeless.

His comment when he viewed the video of his feces-in-their-pants assault was: *God did it.*

MALWARE

I am well aware shiva8843 is your password.

U don't know me and U are wondering why U are getting this mail?

I placed a malware on the adult video clips (pornographic material) website and U visited this site to experience fun (U know what I mean).

While U were watching vids, your internet browser started out working as a RDP with a keylogger which provided me with access to your display screen and web cam.

After that, my software program obtained your entire contacts from your Messenger, Facebook, and e-mail account.

Then I made a double video.

1st part shows the vid U were viewing (you've got cool taste).

2nd part displays the recording of your webcam, yeah its U.

U have 2 choices.

U can ignore this message.

In this scenario, I will send your video recording to every single one of your personal contacts.

The other choice is pay me $2000.

Let us regard it as a donation.

As a result, I most certainly will instantly erase your video recording. U can keep doing your life like this never occurred and U would never hear back again from me.

U will make the payment via Bitcoin (if U do not know this, search "how to buy bitcoin" in Google).

BTC Address:

1ExiUrC3TR6HbYSvp1HVWw8PUv4cSghTC4

[case-sensitive copy, paste it]

U have one day to make the payment.

If I do not receive the Bitcoin, I will send your video to all of your contacts including members of your family, colleagues, etc. Nevertheless, if I receive the payment, I'll erase the video pronto.

This is a nonnegotiable offer.

WORLD IN PAIN

I am the murdered albatross around the mariner's neck

I am the short-handled hoe the bent migrant worker uses

The hangman's noose with clotted blood

The jitterbugging nun

The Muslim child snatched off the street into a "black site"

The sidewinder encoding our grief

The wooden beggar's bowl in Myanmar

The elephant mourning its kin

The brown-skinned pregnant girl shot then dumped into the bloody river

The bridge spanning 8 bloody rivers

The female bear separated from its cubs after the ice splits in the Arctic

The hummingbird brief as your earlobe

The sphinx in a futureless world

I am a triad of words

World in pain

SOURCES

Bangkok Post
BBC
CLG
Al Jazeera
Le Monde
La Prensa
El País
Japan Times
The Intercept
The Free Library
Yahoo & Google
Reuters
The NY Daily News
The Half Moon Bay Review
The Huffington Post
The Atlantic
The Independent UK
The Guardian UK
TruthDig
Mr. S Leather
AlterNet
Intercept
The Village Voice
Rolling Stone
Vanity Fair
The Progressive
Erowid Psychoactive Vaults
Multiple miscellaneous sources on- & off-line

*Epigraph to the volume: The Sirens' song, from Homer's *Odyssey*

A checklist of JEF titles

JEF

Journal of
Experimental
Fiction